The Truth Test

by Lori Pollard-Johnson

For Brian, who gave me the gift of time.

Cover and Inside Illustrations: Margaret Sanfilippo

Text © 2001 by Perfection Learning® Corporation.
Printed in the United States of America. For information, contact
Perfection Learning® Corporation
1000 North Second Avenue, P.O. Box 500
Logan, Iowa 51546-0500
Phone: 1-800-831-4190
Fax: 1-712-644-2392
Paperback ISBN 0-7891-5318-1
Cover Craft® ISBN 0-7807-9694-2
Printed in the U.S.A.
6 7 8 PP 08 07

Contents

1

New Again

Let's get things straight from the start. My name is Jared. Not Jare, not Jerry—it's Jared.

My last name's Springer. No, I'm not related to Jerry Springer, the talk show host.

I'm just Jared Springer. I used to live in Portland, Oregon. Now I'm heading for the Emerald City, otherwise known as Seattle.

The reason for the move is my dad. He's a computer programmer. Actually, he develops computer games, which is pretty cool.

Anyway, he got a job offer from the big M—Microsoft, that is. So we're on our way there now.

My mom is staying in Portland. She's not mad at us or anything like that. She needs to finish her doctoral studies in English literature. She'll be there for a few more months while Dad and I get settled.

This isn't a move I'm very happy about. First of all, I've moved about a zillion times in my 12 years on this planet. Every move was because of my dad's work.

That means about a zillion different schools. And the same questions are asked every time. Somebody asks me where I'm from. Then someone asks if I'm related to Jerry Springer. Sooner or later, someone says something about my weight.

You see, I'm what you'd call *chunky*. I stand 5' 2" tall. I'm never the shortest kid in my class, but never the tallest either.

Now that would be fine if I weighed, say, 90 pounds. It would even be all right if I weighed in at 110. But I tip the scales at 140—on a good day.

I have short, reddish brown hair that looks like a Brillo pad. It's wiry and very curly. My face is round, with about a zillion freckles—more when the sun's out.

My eyes are hazel with brown specks. But no one notices because of my thick glasses.

So I'm quite a sight. My mom tells me I'm a handsome young man. But you know how moms are. They have to say things like that.

I know I look different from a lot of kids. They always notice too. I know Seattle will be no different.

I settled into my chair for my first day at my new Seattle school. I'm a sixth grader. I'm always placed in the accelerated program because I'm supertalented at science—chemistry in particular.

I have my very own chemistry set. I've done many experiments in my spare time. But so far, I haven't blown up anything.

There was one time with my cat—well, actually, her tail. But it was her own fault for hanging around my Bunsen burner.

I was sitting in class when the bell rang. The teacher walked to the front of the room. She adjusted her glasses and took roll.

When she came to my name, she made a big deal about introducing me. I was used to this kind of teacher. This was what I said when she asked me to tell a little about myself.

7

The Truth Test

"My name is Jared—Jared Springer. I'm from Portland, Oregon. But I've lived just about everywhere. So far, Texas has been my favorite. My favorite meal is pizza and root beer. My best subject is science."

I heard laughter from the back of the room. I could have guessed what was said.

It was probably something about how obvious it was that I liked pizza and root beer. Like that's a joke I've never heard before! Yeah, right.

I glanced in that direction. I saw a pretty, blond girl hit a boy on the shoulder. He took it in good stride—a macho man. The teacher shushed them, and we began the day's work.

First up was reading. We read the beginning of an American Indian legend out loud. The teacher asked questions every once in a while.

Halfway through, she told us to finish the story silently. Then we had to answer questions on a worksheet she handed out. The answers had to be in complete sentences.

I finished quickly. It was a good story. It was full of myths about the sun and moon, earthquakes, and animals.

When I handed in my paper, the teacher pointed out a bookshelf. She told me to choose a book to read while waiting.

I found a book on the solar system. This interested me because we'd just read a legend about it. I scooted back to my desk and read until recess.

That's when the trouble began. As soon as I stepped outside, a group formed and headed my direction. That's always the first sign of trouble.

Sure enough, they wanted to ask questions. No, I'm not related to Jerry Springer. No, I don't have a gland problem. I'm just chunky.

There were a few more questions. But I blew them off. Finally, the group left.

When they were gone, I started kicking some dirt clods on the playfield. They broke, crumbling apart. Then I smashed them to dust with my feet. I would like to do that to some of those kids.

Out of the corner of one eye, I saw a kid from my class move in my direction. He wasn't being very direct about it, so I wasn't sure what he wanted yet.

I kept squashing dirt clods. But I was watching him out of the corner of my eye as he wandered my way.

He was a small boy, about half my size. He had fuzzy hair and dark skin. He reminded me of some Hispanic kids I knew in Texas.

I kept working at my dirt-clod activity. He kept getting closer and closer. I considered just asking him what he wanted. But he didn't seem to be bothering anybody, so I kept my mouth shut.

Finally, he was within three feet of me. His face was downcast. His shoulders were hunched, and his hands were in his pockets.

His feet were busy kicking dirt clods. I smiled inwardly. This was the closest I'd had to a friend in three moves.

I backed up a little, seeing a really huge dirt clod. I acted like I was kicking it. But actually, I just pushed it with my foot so it was closer to him.

He saw what I had done and turned his face up. He looked at me and smiled. I smiled back.

We continued on like that, kicking and squashing, until the bell rang. Then we finished the dirt clod we were working on and ran to line up. Mostly, I followed him because he knew where to go and I didn't.

The rest of the day went pretty smoothly. I left people alone. And they left me alone. That suited me fine.

At the end of the day, my teacher, Mrs. Clevenger, asked to talk to me. She told me I'd be going to the accelerated program the next day.

Great, I thought. It would be like doing my first day all over again. There would be more questions and more weight jokes. Great—just great.

2

Honesty

The AFTERS program, Accelerated Formal Talent Education and Recognition Services, met for the full day every Tuesday. It's a stupid title. But most schools I've been to use big words when they don't have to. Anyway, it was pretty fun.

The Truth Test

Since I'm a sixth grader, I got to choose my course of study. Of course, I chose chemistry.

The teacher, Mr. Henderson, found me a desk. Then he showed me two cupboards where the chemistry equipment was kept.

He told me to explore today. Later we'd develop some topics of study. That was cool with me.

I took a quick look in the cupboards. I could see the school had most of the stuff I had at home—a Bunsen burner, glass beakers in several sizes, measuring equipment, a scale, and various chemicals.

I examined each item briefly as I set it on the counter. Then I leaned forward on tiptoes and pulled out four half-filled bottles with handwritten labels.

The labels were dated two years ago. The bottles were labeled *charm*, *beauty*, *honesty*, and *popularity*.

I was curious. So I decided to investigate. I carried the four half-filled bottles over to my desk. Then I went back to the cupboards and put back the items I had taken out.

Instead of stretching to replace the equipment, I climbed onto the counter this time. Now I could see directly into the cupboards. I found a blue notebook with the name *Greta* on the front. Each letter of the name was made with eraser burns.

Now, I knew this was someone else's notebook. And I knew it was private. But this only served to increase my interest.

I glanced over my shoulder, looking around the room. No one noticed me. Careful not to attract attention, I placed the notebook under one knee and set everything back in the cupboard.

I hopped off the counter and closed the cupboard doors. I strolled back to my desk with the notebook tucked under one arm.

I tried to act normal so no one would notice me. I set the notebook down on my desk (with the name facing down) and piled my books on top of it.

I began a full-blown investigation of the bottles first. I've found that if you do something out in the open, people don't notice. It's when you're being sneaky that people pay attention.

First, I picked up the *charm* bottle. I took out a pencil and a sheet of paper and wrote *charm*. I guessed there was about 10 ml in the bottle. I wrote that down on the paper.

Next, I unscrewed the lid on the little bottle. I held it away from me to be safe.

Sometimes chemicals turn weird when left alone. Then they explode when mixed with oxygen. I put on gloves and chemist glasses. Then I took off the lid.

The Truth Test

Nothing happened—no sound, no scent, no visible gasses, no heat reaction. I recorded this data. Then I put the pencil down on the desk and brought the bottle closer to my nose.

I waved one hand back and forth above the bottle. I breathed in softly first. Then I took a deep breath. I still didn't smell anything.

I wrote down this data too. Then I recapped the *charm* bottle and set it back in line with the others.

I continued this way. I wrote down my observations of each of the bottles. There was no real difference among them. They could have been plain old water for all I knew—except for the *honesty* bottle.

It had a clean, minty smell. It was just like my favorite toothpaste that squirts out three colors at once. I made note of *honesty's* scent just as the bell rang for recess.

After recess, we had guided group lessons. So I had to save the notebook until later. When I was safely at home, I could snoop through it.

I felt a little guilty about reading someone else's private thoughts. But I got over it by the time the bell rang.

Over the course of the next few nights, I read what turned out to be Greta's diary and chemistry journal. Between hypotheses, experiments, and results were her thoughts about being a foreign-exchange student.

Listed in the notebook were the problems she had experienced. She also described her feelings. It was sometimes hard to read. She had dealt with a lot of abuse from other students because of her clothing and accent.

Near the end of the journal, I found a list of the chemicals she had mixed in the four bottles. They weren't anything special—just a bunch of harmless chemicals. Most of it was hydrated NaCl—that's just water with salt in it.

I didn't think much about the results of the experiments until the last page. There, she had written her final experiment—transforming herself by drinking the liquid in each bottle.

She had made a record of bodily changes after drinking half of each liquid. There didn't seem to be much change—except a slight stomachache and headache. It made me wonder why she went to such great lengths just to be liked.

The more I wondered, the angrier I got at how hopeless she must have felt. I knew who to blame—the kids who wouldn't leave her alone. It made me so mad!

I carried on with the rest of my week. I thought a lot about Greta and her problems. I didn't come to any satisfactory conclusions, though.

The Truth Test

It wasn't a bad week. In fact, everything went pretty well until Friday. It was on that day that I saw the worst act of school-yard terrorism ever.

It happened when my friend, Marty, and I were walking the track. I had learned that "Marty" was short for Felizio Alfonso Martinez, Jr.

We had gotten into the habit of hanging out together. We didn't say much. But we used the buddy system to get through our miserable sixth-grade recesses.

We were just walking, not even talking, when Brandon decided to join us. Brandon was the biggest, most popular, most smart-mouthed kid in school.

Marty said a quick "hello," but my eyes never lifted from the ground. I knew his visit could only mean trouble.

It didn't take long for Brandon to begin his harassment. Brandon nodded quickly to his buddies at the side of the field. Then he got behind us and imitated our walks.

First he did me. That wasn't very tough. He made a big circle out of his arms and waddled. Ha-ha—real funny.

Next, he got behind Marty and walked zigzag, like Marty was real confused or something. It made me mad—real mad. Marty's not dumb. He just doesn't know the language.

So I turned to Brandon and said, "Why don't you go bother some other Neanderthal?"

He stopped in his tracks and stared at me. "What'd you say, fatboy?"

There was no backing down now. All eyes were on me.

"I said leave us alone and bother someone your own size . . ." I paused a moment, letting that sink through his thick skull. Then I continued, ". . . and mental age."

Brandon was furious. A few of his buddies heard and were laughing. That's the one thing I've noticed about a lot of kids—if they'll laugh at you, they'll laugh at anyone.

Finally, Brandon spoke. "What're you gonna do about it?" he asked. "You gonna roll on me?"

Brandon turned on his heels and faced his buddies. He watched for admiring hoots and hollers.

Now that was a real creative insult. I'd never heard anyone say anything like it before. Yeah, right.

I gathered my courage and took a step toward him. "Go away, moron," I said. My lips curled dangerously.

"Or what?" he demanded. "You gonna hurt me? Oh, I'm so scared. Like anyone's gonna be afraid of a fat, ugly kid like you or your little loser friend. I heard his dad's in jail and his mom can't get a job."

I looked at Marty. His head hung low to the ground. Teardrops fell from his face, landing in a dirty puddle.

I turned toward Marty. Quietly, I said, "Marty, it's okay."

He didn't hear me. Instead, he froze in place. Tears were pouring down his cheeks. I took a step toward him, but he ran off.

I turned to face Brandon again. He was busy high-fiving his buddies, laughing and carrying on. I was so filled with anger that I couldn't do anything but stand there.

When I swung back around to the direction Marty had gone, I could see him run off the school grounds. He ran straight down the street until he was out of sight.

Marty didn't come back that afternoon. He didn't come back the next week either. I figured he was pretty embarrassed.

It didn't matter to me whether any of what Brandon had said was true or not. I just wanted Marty for my friend.

Finally, the following Friday, I asked our teacher where he was. She told me he had left for good.

For the first time in a very long time, I wanted to cry. I wanted to sink to my knees and bawl my eyes out. Partly I was sorry for him. And partly I was sorry for me. I was friendless again.

3

The Test

I lay in bed that night, feeling very sad. I thought about Marty and Brandon. I thought about Greta and her troubles. Then I thought about me—my moves, the rude questions, and the weight jokes.

The Truth Test

Finally, I thought about all the kids who had ever been teased about the way they looked or the way they talked. Suddenly, my sadness gave way to anger. I couldn't get over the unfairness of it all.

Kids like Brandon were everywhere. No one could stop them. I thought about ways I could get Brandon in trouble—telling the teacher or principal, reporting his actions to the police, even suing in court.

None of these ideas would work. They would only make things worse on the playfield the very next day.

The weight of the world was on my short, wide body. I couldn't sleep until I'd solved this problem. About midnight, I figured it out. I had it!

I snapped on the bedside light and wrote down my idea in the notebook. I stored it in my bedside drawer. I wrote . . .

I shut off the light again. I was proud of my idea. The spirit of a million teased 12-year-olds had risen up and spoken to me. Of course! We could outsmart them!

Our brains were our best defense! I was sure I could find a way to beat the Brandons of the world. With thoughts of revenge racing through my mind, I fell asleep.

I got my chance the very next week. While standing in the lunch line, I happened to hear Melissa and Jenny gossiping about another girl. I recognized the girls from my math class.

"Well, she told me she didn't like him," Jenny said.

Now, I didn't care about any of the three girls. But when I heard Melissa say, "Then she must be lying," I couldn't resist.

"You know, girls," I said. I broke into the conversation casually. "There's a way to determine who is telling the truth."

The girls turned and looked at me. They obviously disliked me. But they were interested.

Melissa snapped her gum while Jenny tapped her painted fingertip on her cheek. Jenny looked me up and down. It was as if she could determine my value by my appearance.

"Whaddya mean?" Melissa asked.

"Well," I replied, drawing out the suspense with a pause. "What I mean is, I can tell when people are lying."

Immediately, the girls faced each other. I could tell by the looks on their faces that they were interested. They turned back to me.

Melissa asked, "How do you know?"

I flashed them my best boy-genius grin and thought quickly. What would convince them?

They knew I was terrific in chemistry. That's it—a chemical test! "I've developed a test—a truth test. I did it while I was in the AFTERS program, of course."

The girls eyed me doubtfully. Then they glanced at each other. They seemed to reach some sort of agreement without ever saying a word.

"How's it work?" they asked together.

This was "make-or-break" time for my little game. I straightened the giggle lines from my face and recalled Greta's formulas.

Then I said, "I've created a test that uses saliva. It's simple really. All you need is a little spit from the possible liar and my chemicals. Mix them together and voilá!" I clapped my hands together once for effect.

The girls whispered to each other. This time Melissa twirled a golden lock of hair between two fingers. They were considering the power this test could mean to them.

I grinned with satisfaction. I had pitted the popular crowd against themselves. When the girls turned back around, I could see I had them hooked.

"Okay," they said. "How much?"

"Just $3," I replied. I tried not to smile. But inside, my heart was pounding with excitement.

The girls talked quietly for a minute. Then they pulled out their purses and counted out two crumpled dollar bills and a handful of change.

"Okay, when do we get it?" they asked.

"I'll have it for you by Friday," I said. I did my best not to burst out laughing.

We made plans for the trade-off and parted. I went to my table by the window where I sat alone. They joined the "in" crowd.

I couldn't help but feel proud. At long last, I had beaten them at their own game.

I tinkered with my chemistry set all night. Around 1 a.m., I found a substance that would turn pink when mint was detected.

There was no scientific reason I decided to use mint as the tattletale factor. I thought about Greta's experiments. And I figured with all the gum and breath sweeteners those girls eat, there would be a lot of mint in their spit. Also, I had a large supply of minty toothpaste to use in my research.

I brought the chemicals to school in a small packet. I gave it to the girls at the agreed-upon time.

"Listen, this better work," Melissa said. She flipped her hair back over her shoulder. " 'Cause if it doesn't, I'm gonna tell Brandon."

"Yeah," Jenny chimed in. "And if it does work, you'd better be ready to make us some more."

With that, the two girls stalked away. They were off to find the supposed liar and get to the bottom of things.

I chuckled, looking forward to what would happen next. Only for a moment did I feel somewhat responsible for what was sure to come. I pushed the guilt away quickly, though. I really believed they deserved whatever happened.

Besides, what's the worst that could come of it? They'd argue even more about whether the truth test works or not. And the rest of us would be in for some cheap fun at their expense. Me—I'd be laughing all the way to the bank.

That didn't happen.

Instead, the truth test worked. The girl's truth test came up positive, and everyone believed it.

Word spread that I had invented the test. By the end of the day, I had four more orders. They were all students claiming to care about the truth. Yeah, right.

I thought about my future. I decided to make as much money off this little scam as I could. I filled the orders and held my breath as the test declared honesty and lies. Then I took my money and opened up a savings account.

What surprised me most was the kids' complete belief in the test. No matter what the test said, they believed it over their own friends.

If I'd considered the consequences, I would have stopped. I didn't, though. And all of a sudden, I was on a wild roller coaster ride with no end in sight.

4

Trouble with
the Test

All of a sudden, I was Mr. Popularity. Friends came out of the woodwork to be near me.

In music class, the coolest kids sat by me. At recess, I couldn't get away by myself. And I was forever being sent notes by classmates.

Trouble with the Test

My only relief came on Tuesdays, when I escaped to the AFTERS program. No one there knew I was the inventor of the truth test. They thought of me as the new kid who liked chemistry. It felt good not to be recognized.

On Wednesdays, though, I returned to the classroom. There would be a dozen notes on my desk, held down with a painted rock paperweight. Most of the notes would be orders for more truth tests.

A couple would be notes asking me who I liked. My answer was always the same. I didn't like any of the girls in a special way.

Partly I was pleased with my new popularity. It felt good to be one of the group—even if it was to be short-lived. I knew it could be over in an instant. This simply couldn't go on forever.

I was making a lot of money too. At about ten tests a week, I'd made $120 in only one month.

Every time I made a deposit, I smiled with satisfaction. I knew I'd used my brain to get even with the very kids who had humiliated Marty, Greta, and me. It was so easy.

There was a tricky situation one day when the result of a truth test showed a boy to be a liar. He refused to back down. I noticed the noise and listened in.

"You told me you'd bring my dad's baseball mitt back the next day!" one boy charged. "Then you claimed you were sick and couldn't come over. Then I got in trouble!"

"I was sick!" the second boy claimed. "Even ask my mom. This truth test lies!"

I had heard enough. I knew it was time to step in and smooth things over.

"Sometimes," I said, breaking into the uneasy group, "you can experience a false negative. This appears to be one of those times. Let me check the packet. If it's a bad batch, I'll replace the truth test with another one for free."

This calmed the group. And they still believed in the truth test.

"Yeah, okay," the boys mumbled together.

Again, I was the hero. It was easy staying a hero once you were there. The hard part was getting there.

By the end of the fifth week, the truth test was totally trusted again. But I was getting way too many orders. The sixth graders couldn't be using all of them. And it concerned me.

Then Brandon's right-hand man, Joshua, came over to order four tests. I asked him who they were for.

"See, dude," he began, "my brother's in eighth grade and his girlfriend's telling people she wants to break up with him. But whenever my brother asks her about the rumor, she denies it. He needs to check out her story. That way, he can break up with her first." He made a fist and pounded the air to show support for his brother.

"Okay," I said. I didn't really see the harm in selling a few tests to older kids as well. I was feeling good about my plan. What could go wrong now?

"I'll have it by Monday," I told him.

And so it went. I'd collect my fees, make a deposit, buy more chemicals, and make more truth tests. Then I'd bring them to school where kids almost ripped the little packets out of my hands.

The trouble began only two weeks later. Word had spread about my truth test. Now kids from the junior high just down the street were making the trip to buy my test.

They walked right onto the school grounds and asked for me by name. Then they placed their orders.

I had a funny feeling about this. But I shrugged it off. I was making a lot of money and having a great time.

Pulling the plug on the whole deal now would make me unpopular again. I couldn't do that. No sixth grader in his right mind would.

So I kept filling orders. But the more orders that came in, the more uneasy I felt. I tried hard to ignore it.

The Truth Test

Then the high school kids began to order the truth test. I realized the whole thing had gotten out of hand. I found myself wishing I'd never thought up this trick.

Yet, how could I stop? I considered talking to the counselor at school. That wouldn't do. I'd have to give the money back.

I thought about asking my dad for advice. But I realized he'd want me to give the money back too.

I'd saved a lot of the money. But I'd also spent some on chemistry equipment and producing the little packets—as well as some on great computer games. I was stuck.

After many hours of thinking about my problem, I thought of a plan. I'd tell my customers that I lost the formula.

I'd explain how the recipe got too close to the Bunsen burner and caught fire. I'd tell them there was nothing left but ashes. I practiced in the mirror, saying each word again and again until it was stuck in my memory.

Once I was sure it was perfect, I felt really good. Sure, I'd go back to being just Jared Springer. I'd probably even be teased again. That was okay—at least I'd be out of the hot seat.

Unfortunately, good ideas often come too late. When I got to school the next day, a newspaper reporter was waiting for me. He wanted to hear my story. My heart sank.

I was pointed in his direction. All I could see was a mob of kids, most of them my customers, surrounding him. As I got nearer, I could hear them telling their tales of "truth found out."

"It really works!" they cried.

I turned to walk away. I may not be able to resist easy popularity, but I'm smart enough to know what Abe Lincoln said is still true.

"You can fool some of the people all the time, and all of the people some of the time. But you cannot fool all of the people all the time."

5

In the News

Holding my breath, I walked quietly away. I must have taken ten steps when I heard it.

"There he is!" someone called out. Caught! And no wonder! How many other truth-test inventors were there in the school?

I couldn't ignore him. What was I going to do?

I decided to buy time. I pretended not to hear him. That worked for about three seconds. Then Brandon raced up to me.

"Hey, Jare, buddy," he sang out. He threw an arm around my shoulders as if we were the best of friends.

I glanced up but kept walking. "How's it going, Brandon?" I replied.

"Listen, Jerry. This guy from the paper wants to talk to you," he said. "You know, about the truth test."

I frowned. Behind him, the crowd was quickly approaching. I'd have to come up with something quick. But what?

I urged my brain to come up with a plan that would be truthful and keep me from being beaten up. With this much pressure, though, I couldn't think straight. My hands started to sweat, and a flash flood drenched my armpits.

Folding my arms over my chest, I hid the sweat stains under my arms. This also served to keep my stomach from exploding as butterflies flapped their wings inside. What to do? What to do?

All the while, the reporter and kids moved closer. I felt like I couldn't breathe. In a second, they caught up with Brandon and me.

"Hello, Jared," the man said. He stuck out his right hand while holding his notepad and pen in his left. I took his hand shyly and shook it. I hoped he didn't notice the sweat.

"I hear you're the inventor of the truth test," he said as he shook my hand.

I nodded.

The man grinned. "I was wondering if you'd like to tell us a little about how you developed it—maybe share the formula?"

The man winked at me and flipped open his notepad. He clicked the top of his pen three times. He was waiting for me to speak.

"Well, I . . ." I began.

"That's okay. I can see you don't want to share the formula," he said, winking again. "I understand it's a trade secret and all. Just tell me how it works."

I looked around. Everyone who had ever bought a test from me was there. They were waiting for my answer.

I couldn't get out of this situation gracefully. I had to say something.

Now, I knew from past experience that when fibbing, the best policy is to keep the story simple. Keep it as close as possible to actual events. That way you can remember what was said in case someone asks in the future.

"Well . . ." I began. I gathered up my courage and put on a brave front. "It began in chemistry class."

The man nodded. He scribbled a note. "Go on," he said, encouraging me.

"I found a notebook with some experiments done by a former student in the AFTERS program." I looked around. All eyes were on me. They were listening and believing every word I said.

"She had developed some liquids that promised positive traits—one of which was honesty." I paused a moment, catching my breath. The crowd moved closer.

"I carried on with her idea," I continued. "And I added my own stuff where necessary."

"How so?" the reporter asked. His eyebrows rose with his question.

How indeed? I went blank. Then I had a brainstorm—*Jurassic Park*.

"Kind of like in *Jurassic Park*," I continued, not missing a beat. "They took the DNA from a fossilized critter in amber. Then they filled in with animal DNA from today."

The man paused and looked down at me. He was probably a good foot taller than me. Right now, it seemed like his eyes bore down from about ten feet above my head.

His pen went still. He looked straight into my eyes, holding my stare a moment longer than normal. Amusement entered his expression. A split second later, his eyes shifted focus.

He knows I'm lying, I thought. I waited to see what he would do.

He stared at me a moment longer. I knew he was trying to decide whether to tell everyone the truth. He swung his gaze around the group before settling on me again.

My heart dropped to my knees, which immediately went weak. He could ruin my life with a few words.

Then, it was a miracle! He grinned.

The reporter double-clicked his pen. He said, "Go on."

I continued with my story. I was obviously pulling a lot of fuzzy white wool over my friends' eyes. The reporter listened halfheartedly to my tale. He nodded from time to time. But he rarely wrote down anything else I said.

I sighed inwardly. If he intended to blow my cover, he would already have done so.

When I finished, he asked if the kids would head back to class. He wanted to talk to me alone.

The crowd left. He put away his notepad and pen. He stared at me. I smiled weakly.

"Jared, why did you do this?" he asked. There was no beating around the bush with this guy.

"What do you mean?" I replied. I knew he knew. But I didn't know if he knew that I knew he knew.

He continued staring. I shifted my weight uneasily.

"You know what I mean," he said.

"Well," I began, looking down at my feet, "I did it because they're mean. They were rude to me, to Marty, and to Greta." I raised my eyes to meet his.

"They deserved it," I said. I tipped my chin up. I dared him to argue with me.

The reporter tilted his head back. He studied the clouds. "Jared," he said seriously. His eyes were still focused on the sky. "I'm not going to report this story. I can't say that I admire what you've done to these kids, but I do understand.

"Twenty years ago, I was where you are," the reporter continued. "I was teased because my brother was retarded. People would point and laugh. No one wanted to come over and spend the night. A few even spread rumors that I would become just like him. They said I would be stuck in a wheelchair and wear a bib to keep my own drool off me."

The reporter looked at me. "Believe me when I say it doesn't go on forever. Eventually, you'll go to high school and then college. While those people will still be around, there will be fewer of them. You won't have to deal with their rudeness as often."

He straightened his back. I was quiet.

"You obviously have a gift for tricking people," he said. A quick smile formed at his mouth. "But people will find out. You'd better plan how you're going to handle things when they do."

The Truth Test

The reporter turned to go. Then he swung back around. He looked at me and winked. Then he patted my shoulder once. After that, he was on his way.

"Thanks," I called out a second later. His response was a quick wave. I was glad he had killed the story. And I also felt better about the future.

It's hard to believe when you're in the middle of sixth grade that *everyone* gets teased. But it's true. If it's not your weight, it's the color of your hair or the clothes you wear. Sometimes, it's things you can't ever change—like your nationality, your height, or the people in your family.

I thought about these things. Maybe we all have something that's not quite perfect about ourselves. But I also figured we all must have something that is perfect too.

Inspired, I began to believe there was life after sixth grade.

6
The Real Truth

I thought about the reporter's words all day long—
on the bus ride home and after dinner until late in the
evening. I didn't even play my new computer game,
Insect Armageddon.

I had too much to think about. On the one hand, I was very grateful that the newspaper reporter hadn't revealed my secret.

On the other hand, his parting statement really bothered me. He was right. It was only a matter of time before people found out.

In fact, I think I've known all along someone would figure it out. At the time, though, I didn't care. I just wanted revenge.

I also didn't think the fallout would happen so soon. I was definitely not ready for the anger that was sure to come my way.

I chewed on the problem again in bed. I carefully considered my choices. I could make up more lies that would explain the truth test. I could admit what I'd done. Or I could move far away.

The last choice would be the easiest. However, I knew my dad would never go for it. He and my mom would get together and want to *discuss* it.

Then they'd wave the "do-what's-right" flag. I'd be forced to admit my lies to everyone. If I was going to do that, I might as well go for the second choice and save myself some time. After all, the result would be the same—getting beat up by Brandon the Big Ape.

I couldn't think of a solution. Then I remembered the last time I had a brainstorm was right before I drifted into REM. That's *Rapid Eye Movement* sleep— when it's hard to wake people up.

I needed to sleep. I wanted to free my mind of the stress. Then I'd find an answer.

Fortunately, my tiredness from the events of the day worked in my favor. I was very tired. I concentrated on the gentle pit-a-pat of rain against my window until I fell asleep.

When I awoke, I hadn't solved anything. The sky was gray—not a speck of sunlight shone through. I got up, padded over to my window, and looked out.

Gray on the street. Gray on the sidewalk. Gray in the sky.

Puddles on the ground. Puddles on my window. Puddles on the leaves.

I looked up into the morning sky. There was more rain. It was very gloomy. Of all the places I'd ever lived, Seattle had to be the wettest and most dismal.

The weather outside did nothing to inspire me. I was no closer to a solution to this big mess than I had been last night.

I arrived at school soaked—except for my head. That's the good thing about Brillo pad hair. Nothing gets through!

A few steps into the hallway, it all began.

"Hey, Jared," Melissa said, "looks like you're messed up." She snapped her gum. I wondered how on earth she got away with chewing so much gum in a strict, no-gum school.

Before I could reply, Joshua spoke up. "My brother used that truth test on his girlfriend. It said she was telling the truth, but she wasn't. My brother got dumped, anyway," he snarled. "And it's all because of you!"

I was speechless. I simply had no words for what was happening. I went through all the former explanations in my head and began.

"Maybe it was that particular test," I said. "I could—"

I was interrupted by Brandon. "Look, you little pig, everyone's on to you now. Jenny gave one of your truth tests to her sister who's in college. She tested it. And it doesn't work."

Brandon glared at me. It was obvious I was about to be hit. Now I've never actually been beat up before, but I was sure it would involve fists. And here I was without my boxing gloves.

Jenny started in. "Yeah, Jar-ed," she said. She drew out my name as a taunt. "My sister's studying chemistry. She's really good at it—better than you. She says your truth test doesn't work."

Jenny slowed a moment. She flipped her ponytail over her shoulder with one hand. Her fingertips were painted blue with a big, fat sun in the middle of each one. Crossing her arms in front of her, she finished, "And I believe her."

Now I knew it was over. I looked around me. I wasn't sure how to handle this.

I tried to create a new lie to cover the old one. But I realized I'd just be continuing in the lie spiral. Once a lie begins, it has to continue on forever or else it unravels. But I wasn't ready to tell the truth either.

"You're just a liar!" one kid yelled from the back. Shouts of agreement followed.

My head dropped to my chest. They had figured it out. Worst of all, I still had no idea how to handle it.

"I know," Melissa said, snapping a particularly large bubble. "Let's show him how it feels."

She searched the crowd for encouragement. More than a few heads nodded their support. So she announced, "Let's make him take the truth test!"

I couldn't believe that with the evidence they had against me, they could have any doubt. But they still weren't sure.

They wanted me to take the truth test to see if I was for real. It was the dumbest idea I'd ever heard. They would trust my answer even though I was the person they thought was lying.

As crazy as it sounds, I started to feel sorry just then. At first, I had only felt happy tricking these popular people. Then I was afraid of getting beat up when everyone found out.

Now, I felt guilt. I took advantage of these kids.

That made me think. Maybe I judged these kids too harshly. True, they were mean to people like Greta, Marty, and me. For that, they deserved a small payback.

But they probably didn't deserve as much payback as I had given them. Their whole world had been turned upside down.

When I thought about how much money I had taken from them, I felt like a con artist. I had profited from my trick. That was wrong.

Now, they wanted me to take the test myself. They thought somehow that would prove whether I was lying about the test. It was absolutely unreal!

And then, I knew what I had to do. I would tell the truth about the truth test.

"Okay," I began. My heart pounded as I looked at each and every one of them. "Let me say first that I'm sorry. I know you are all upset with me and my test. I know what I did to all of you was wrong . . ."

"What about our money, fat boy?" a voice interrupted. The crowd cheered in agreement.

"I will pay you all back as soon as possible," I said. "I've spent a lot of the money. But I'll go to my dad and see if he'll help pay you back."

That seemed to calm the crowd for about 30 seconds. Then, they began fighting over who was owed the most money. Since there was nothing left for me to do, I left the crowd.

Their voices grew louder as I moved farther from the group. I had just reached the classroom door when a hand on my shoulder stopped me. I turned, fully expecting to be hit. Instead, it was Jenny.

Her eyes looked straight into my own. She asked, "Just tell me one thing, Jared. Why did you do this to us?"

I paused. The disappointment I felt in myself made my reasons foggy. I thought back to that first day I had overheard her and Melissa talking in the lunch line.

I remembered some of the words they had used and their all-knowing tone of voice. I felt myself get angry all over again.

"Because of the way you treat people," I said, staring back at her. "Because of the way you and your friends treat Marty and kids like him. Because of the way you made fun of me."

Her blue eyes shone clear with understanding. She stared at me—and I at her—a moment longer. Then we both lowered our gazes. We stood there, not really having anything more to say.

She'd made her point. I'd made mine. They were both true. And we both knew it.

7

Doing the Right Thing

I told my dad that night. Sometimes he's busy and doesn't listen carefully to me. Tonight, though, he paid special attention to my problem.

He asked all the fatherly questions. "Why?" "How much money do you owe?" "How'd you come up with such an idea?"

I answered each question honestly. My pride had long since disappeared. Then my dad said something that made me feel better.

"I don't like what you did or why you did it, Jared," he said. "But I do like you."

Tears formed in my eyes at his words. I'd done a truly awful thing—about as bad as what those kids had done to me. But my dad still loved me. At that moment, that was all that mattered.

Now, my dad isn't especially good with tears—just ask my mom. He fidgets and avoids eye contact when people cry in front of him. Tonight was no different.

When he saw the tears in my eyes, he started to squirm. I was embarrassed too. Then he surprised me again. He put down his fork, pushed back his chair, and came around to my side.

Wrapping his arms around me, he told me that everything was going to be all right. He said that part of this was his fault—his and my mom's—for moving me so many times. And he knew he wasn't around as much as I needed.

I corrected him. This was my fault—only mine.

Oddly enough, I felt better. It was as if by telling my dad, my problem was solved.

I slept well that night—better than I had in a long time. The next morning I arrived early at school with little forms I'd printed on my computer the evening before. I passed one out to every kid who had bought my truth test.

I explained how to fill them out. I told kids that when I got the forms back, I would refund their money. I had a pretty good idea how much I owed, but not the exact amount.

By the end of the day, I had several forms back. At home, I added up the money and showed it to my dad. He gasped a couple times. Then he reminded me that he would take the money out of my allowance for as long as it took to pay him back.

He pulled out the cash. As promised, he had gone to the bank and asked for a lot of $1 bills.

He kept one copy of the receipts, so he'd know how much I owed him. I attached the total number of dollar bills to be refunded to a second copy.

I kept a third copy in my room. It's always good to have a record of who you paid, how much, and when. It's especially important when you're dealing with cash.

The rest of the week continued that way. I would pass out forms to kids who heard about the refund policy. They would fill them out. And I would bring the cash back to school the next day.

It felt good. I felt like I'd finally put down a huge weight I'd been carrying.

Just when everything was going smoothly, Mrs. Clevenger asked to see me during recess. As the kids left the room, I wasted time with my books. I took an extra long time to put away my pencil and eraser in their carrying case.

When everyone was gone, I approached Mrs. Clevenger's desk. "You wanted to see me, Mrs. Clevenger?"

"Yes, Jared," she said. "Please have a seat." She nodded her head toward the chair that sat next to her desk. I sat down.

"Jared, I've noticed there have been a lot of . . . transactions recently," she paused a moment. She glanced at me quickly and then continued. "I'm wondering why so much money is changing hands."

She stopped shortly. It was obviously my turn.

"Well," I started. It had been hard enough admitting what I'd done to the kids. And it had been even tougher to tell my dad.

Telling a teacher, though, was the worst— especially when she made decisions on grades and whether or not I could continue in the AFTERS program.

I hung my head and spilled the story. I didn't raise my eyes once. I told her about the teasing, about Greta, then Marty, and myself.

I explained how I'd come up with the idea. I even answered all the questions Dad had asked before she even had a chance to ask them. I finished in silence.

Mrs. Clevenger was quiet a moment. She was deep in thought. I waited. I thought she'd begin a lecture about school-yard ethics, forgiveness, and maturity.

But it didn't come. After a minute or two of quiet, she excused me from the classroom and told me to enjoy recess. I couldn't figure her out. But I did as I was told.

I found out the next week what her silence meant. Not because she told me, though. Instead, I figured it out from her lesson on Monday morning.

She began by talking about expectations— expectations of sixth graders, expectations of seventh graders, and expectations of human beings.

She asked us why we have laws. We answered "because there are things people shouldn't do."

She questioned us about mores. No one knew what those were. So she explained.

"Mores are customs, like manners, of a group of people. Here's a good example. Why do people stand in line at the movie theater?" she asked.

Instantly, hands shot up. Mrs. Clevenger pointed to a girl in the back row.

"Because it's neat and orderly?" She said it like it was a question. But we all knew it was right.

"Yes," agreed Mrs. Clevenger. "But why do we value orderliness in public places? Why don't we just let the bigger people budge their way to the front of the line to get their tickets first? Why don't we just push a child or someone in a wheelchair out of the way?"

More hands went up. Again, Mrs. Clevenger pointed—this time to a boy in front. I knew him from the AFTERS program. He's smaller than the average sixth grader and superthin.

"Because it's not fair!" he said.

Mrs. Clevenger put on her surprised face. "Why do we care about doing what's fair?" she asked.

No hands went up this time. Fairness is important. No one would disagree with that. *Why* is it so important? That's a harder thing to explain.

Realizing that no one wanted to answer the question, Mrs. Clevenger asked some leading questions. Those are questions teachers use to get a certain answer. I didn't volunteer an answer.

I knew what she was getting at. She was trying to teach the class morality—and what it had to do with the truth test. She wanted us to understand our role in the whole mess. No one was free of guilt.

After what seemed like forever, she summed it up. "We do what is fair because that is what's right. We are not animals. We are able to consider someone else's situation and act as we should. Maybe that is to help someone else. Maybe it is to teach something."

Mrs. Clevenger paused and then continued. "Whatever the reason, however, we do it because no one among us is perfect. We know that. We also know that everyone has gifts and challenges. Some gifts and challenges you can see. Some you cannot see. Seeing that we all succeed and suffer makes us human. That is a good thing because it makes us better people. And better people make a better world."

When she finished, she looked around the room. Everyone was quiet. Something about her words and her strong feelings made us listen carefully. No one spoke out.

I kept my eyes on Mrs. Clevenger. I knew all this was because of the truth-test mess.

After a moment of unusual peace in the classroom, Mrs. Clevenger glanced at the clock. She announced that she would be reading from a very famous book called *How to Win Friends and Influence People*. It was written by a guy named Dale Carnegie.

She held up the book. It was about a zillion years old. Opening to page one, she began with a story about the importance of remembering someone's name.

I listened. The rest of the class did too.

Surprisingly, at recess, there were fewer put-downs. It could have been just my imagination—maybe not. Things did seem to get easier for me, though. And I was grateful for that.

8
Surprises

The next couple of weeks I returned to being a normal kid. Everyone had been paid back. And the total refund was about what I figured it should be.

Surprise! No one had tried to rip me off. Maybe Mrs. Clevenger's little morality lessons were working.

The Truth Test

One day, Mrs. Clevenger was reading us a tale about making friends. In the middle of the story, we had a surprise.

The intercom buzzed. A request for me to go to the school office came over the speaker.

All eyes turned toward me. I blushed. I looked at Mrs. Clevenger. She nodded. I got up and walked straight to the office.

Mrs. Harper, the principal, greeted me herself. I was invited into her office. There was a smile on her face.

I didn't think I was in trouble. But you just never know.

A man dressed in a suit and tie sat in her office. He grinned at me too. Instantly, my palms, feet, and armpits began to sweat.

Mrs. Harper pointed to a chair. I sat in it.

"Jared," Mrs. Harper said, "this is Dr. Patel. He is from the University of Washington's chemistry department."

Suddenly, I knew why I was invited to this little get-together. "I can explain," I said. "I made the fake test. But I paid everybody back." I was breathing really hard. I couldn't get much else out.

"No, no," Dr. Patel said. "I don't care about that." He spoke with a thick Indian accent. So I had to listen carefully. I turned to face him, concentrating on his words.

"One of my sophomore students brought this little test to me. She's a brilliant girl." He glanced in Mrs. Harper's direction.

Then he looked back at me. A grin spread across his warm brown skin.

"Of course, the test does not work like it was supposed to. There is no way to determine truth from saliva . . . *that we know of so far*." He emphasized those words. Scientists have to be open to new ideas.

"Now, we know there are tribes—in Africa, for example—that have a sort of saliva test that determines honesty. In their culture, when there has been a dishonest act, they place a long, wood-handled knife into the fire. When it's hot, they line up all the members of the community. They touch the tip of the red-hot knife onto the tongue of each person."

His speech left me dizzy. I was unsure why he was telling me all this. I snuck a peek at Mrs. Harper.

She was listening closely. I figured she wanted to know what the point to this little tale was too.

I shifted my attention back to Dr. Patel. He just kept on talking.

"Of course, the tribal members have complete faith in this test. So it works," he continued.

"Wouldn't their tongues get burned?" I asked. I couldn't help being curious.

"Good question, Jared," Dr. Patel responded. "You see, when people are relaxed, they have plenty of saliva on their tongue. This prevents burning from the quick touch of a hot item. People who are under a lot of stress have little saliva. So they are burned when the knife is held against their tongue. Everyone knows their guilt and the 'trial' is over."

Dr. Patel clapped his hands together. He was pleased with his story. "It works every time," he ended.

The room was quiet a moment. Then Dr. Patel said, "Oh, my reason for visiting today. It seems my student, Karen, got one of these tests from her sister. Her sister is your friend, Jennifer," he said.

I couldn't help but laugh. Like I was *friends* with any of those kids now.

Dr. Patel held open his suit jacket with one hand. Then he reached into his pocket with the other. He pulled out an envelope and handed it to me.

"In that envelope, Jared, you will find two things. The first is a check for $500. The second is a $500 scholarship to the University of Washington. The scholarship will be good should you decide to study there."

My hands trembled. My heart raced. Could what he said be true? Gently, I opened the envelope. Sure enough, there was a check inside for $500!

Next to it, there was a letter. It was addressed to me. The letter explained my scholarship.

Why on earth was I given this money? I started to question him. Dr. Patel stopped me with one hand raised.

"You see, Jared, while your test failed as a truth test, Karen discovered she could separate mint from alcohol.

This technology will give police officers a faster means of determining whether drivers have hidden alcohol with gum or mints before getting into their cars. That could be very important."

Dr. Patel paused a moment. He let his words sink in. "When Karen figured this out, she brought it to me and explained how she had gotten the test. We originally gave her $1000 with a $1000 scholarship. But she said you deserved half. So I'm here to give it to you." Dr. Patel crossed one leg over the other and settled back in his chair.

I was speechless. I managed to mutter a "thanks," but that's about all. Dr. Patel left then.

Mrs. Harper told me I could use her phone. She thought I might want to call my parents and share the great news. Mrs. Harper got Dad's work number from her files.

I called and was rewarded with excited questions. Dad also promised dinner out and an ice cream dessert.

Also, he told me I had another big surprise. Mom was coming home tonight.

We celebrated over banzai burgers. Those are hamburgers with a slice of pineapple between the patty and the bun.

We helped ourselves to seconds on the refillable baskets of french fries. Then Dad and I ordered the mile-high mud pie.

The Truth Test

Everything was delicious! But we had to hold our stomachs as we walked back to our car. We were stuffed!

Mom's plane was due at Sea-Tac Airport in a little under an hour. So we made our way there. We wanted to watch her plane land.

I've always loved airports. It's incredible to watch giant metal machines take off and land. Sure, I understand the physics behind it. My dad explained it to me. It always amazes me, though.

Mom's plane taxied across the tarmac. My heart soared. I hadn't really realized how much I missed her until now.

I stood next to the glass wall. I watched as the workers attached the plane to the airport tunnel.

Suddenly, the doors flew open. People started pouring out. I moved closer to the doors.

There's one thing I've noticed about airports. Every kind of person spills from them.

Before Mom got off the plane, I saw women in saris and men in turbans. There were tall men made taller with cowboy boots and ten-gallon hats.

I also saw a woman juggling two babies and a piece of luggage. She was enthusiastically greeted by a man near the back.

Then, like magic, there was my mom. She was wearing sweats—her favorite flying clothes. She carried her purse over her shoulder and a book in one hand.

"Mom," I called out.

About 30 women's heads turned in my direction. They were all responding to my one-word greeting. My mom looked too.

"Jared!" she exclaimed, rushing toward me. She held her arms out in front of her. I rushed forward and hugged her.

She hugged Dad next. Then we went down to the baggage claim. We got her luggage and piled into our car for the drive home.

Dad made me tell her about the truth test myself. She didn't seem too upset. I must have caught her at a good time.

She didn't scold me or say she was disappointed. Probably because I'd already solved the problem. And the scholarship made everything better.

When we got home, I gave her the $500 check. And I showed her my copies of all the money I had paid back to students. She promised to open a savings account with whatever was left after paying Dad back.

She was surprised at how well we had held things together. I told her it was great to be together again. I really meant it.

9
Cougarland

The next couple of months went pretty well. I steered clear of trouble and the Brandon crowd. I focused on my studies.

I also won first place in my school's science fair. I used lemon juice to power a string of Christmas lights. It took 17 lemons, all lined up, and copper wires. But finally it worked.

Everyone was really impressed with the way I'd used an ordinary food to power the lights. Even a couple of kids from class came up and complimented me on my project.

For the next two weeks, I tinkered with lemon power. I was trying to find the number of lemons I would need to power my video games.

Unfortunately, my tests were interrupted when Mom caught me slipping three crates of lemons into her grocery cart. Video games require a huge amount of lemon energy!

All in all, things were going pretty well. Then spring hit—which meant spring vacation.

Now, I need to explain something about my parents. Every spring, for as long as I can remember, we've taken a trip. This time, they decided we needed to spend some time in the woods by Mount Rainier.

My mom painted word pictures for me—a rustic cabin, evergreens, wildflowers. Dad added to the picture—no electricity, wildlife, using our wits to survive. It's lovely this time of year, they assured me.

It sounded dull. But I agreed, anyway.

Gadgetless, we packed up my mom's Saturn station wagon. And away we went! We inched our way out of Seattle—along with a zillion other cars piled high with kids and luggage.

Most of the other kids looked bored already. I thought I could see one kid asking "How much longer?" about ten miles south of the city.

I flipped on my battery-powered Gameboy. I turned off the sound. My parents had said no electrical stuff. They didn't say no battery stuff.

The next time I looked up, I saw flat green stretches of land. I watched out the window awhile.

I took in the endless branches until the four-lane road gave way to two lanes. Soon, trees and clumps of wildflowers grew alongside the road.

We've never lived far from a city. Mom always needed to be close to the college she was attending. Dad always had to be near work. So seeing all these trees was pretty weird—but pretty wonderful too.

We stopped at a country gas station. We asked directions to Waterton. It was the nearest town to the cabin we had rented for the weekend.

They gave us a map and good directions. For the most part, I ignored the conversation. Then I caught the word *cougar*.

My ears perked up. The gas station attendant was talking. He wore blue overalls and a cap. He had stains on his hands.

"Yeah, they've had a few cougar sightings out in that area," he said. "They don't go after kids much. But if you have any pets with you, you might think about keeping them on a leash."

COUGARS! I glanced at my mom. I figured she'd be worried.

Instead, she wore an amused, interested grin. I turned my attention back to the man. He had finished pumping the gas into our car. Now he was getting the money from Dad.

Dad followed the attendant's directions out of the gas station's driveway. I stared at him. He was smiling.

Here we were—in the middle of nowhere. Cougars were on the loose. And he's grinning like this is the best adventure he's ever had!

He turned to my mom and said, "Maybe we'll have a cougar sighting." Then he reached over and took my mom's hand.

Mom said, "Maybe so." She squeezed my dad's hand.

I couldn't believe it. It was sickening watching my parents snuggle. I went back to my Gameboy.

Another hour passed. My dad announced, "We're here!"

I looked up from my Gameboy. I glanced out the window. I saw we were traveling on a skinny, two-lane road.

A huge logging truck came at us from the opposite direction. He whizzed past us. He gave us a little wave as he went by.

All I could do was stare. I wondered how they got those huge, heavy logs onto a truck!

Up ahead, I saw a stone arch with words carved into the rocks at the top.

I looked up ahead. I was looking for the city that would deserve such a large sign.

I saw a gas station and read the sign.

CARL'S
Last Gas Before the Mountain

Then there was a four-sided building with a billboard out front.

Mabel's Home Cooking

First I glanced at the gas gauge. Did we have enough gas to outrun the cougars?

Then I heard my stomach rumble. It had been six hours since we had last eaten.

"Let's stop for something to eat," Mom said. It was as if she could read my mind—or my stomach.

Dad pulled the station wagon into Mabel's parking lot—all four stalls. We got out of the car.

I looked around. I didn't see any cougars. But then, cougars probably don't walk the streets. Do they?

Mom and Dad loved Mabel's diner. They loved the country charm.

"A person could really relax out here," Dad said. I rolled my eyes. It's a typical 12-year-old skill I've recently perfected.

I ate a surprisingly good turkey club sandwich and french fries. We finished our meal and continued on our way.

I watched out the window for the rest of the trip. If there was going to be a cougar sighting, I was not going to miss it.

We drove several miles. Then we turned onto a one-lane road. There were very few houses around.

Finally, that road gave way to a dirt road. I felt my stomach jump. We were almost there! I thought.

That wasn't true. We continued on for a long time. Our car bumped and jumped with every pothole on this old road. We were on this road for exactly 54 minutes.

The Truth Test

We crossed over a one-lane, wooden bridge that looked a zillion years old. It must have been made for horses and buggies.

I shut my eyes tight as we squeaked over the bridge. I dared to open them only when I felt all four tires grind dirt. We rounded a bend and then we were there.

Dad parked in front of the cabin. Cautiously, I looked around. I didn't see any cougars.

I followed him into the cabin, carrying my stuff. There was one bedroom, a kitchen, and a living room. The living room had a couch and bookshelf. It looked comfortable.

The kitchen was another story. There was no microwave, refrigerator, or oven. All it had was a sink, some cupboards, and a grill that vented outside.

Mom and Dad practically hummed with delight. They set about putting the ice chest in the kitchen and cleaning the grill.

When they finished, we built a fire in the pit outside. We roasted hot dogs and made s'mores. The moon came out. It was followed by about a zillion stars.

I lay between Mom and Dad on a sleeping bag we spread out on the dirt. We shared a large pillow, tucked under our heads.

Staring at the stars, we made out the Big Dipper

and Little Dipper. I didn't know enough about astronomy to pick out anything else.

We spent a thoroughly enjoyable week just hiking and talking and roasting marshmallows. Three times, deer wandered into our cabin's front yard. We huddled next to the window to watch them as they grazed.

We didn't see any other people—or cougars.

Late Sunday afternoon, we piled back into our station wagon for the ride back. We stopped at Mabel's for sodas to go.

Just on the outskirts of Seattle, Mom turned to Dad and said something strange.

"I think I could do it," she said. A relaxed smile spread across her face.

Dad grinned back at her. "Me too."

I looked up. What was this? "What's going on?" I asked.

With a nod from Dad, Mom spilled it. She told me about her job offer to teach online courses. And she explained about Dad working at home from now on.

Then I understood. We were moving again—to Cougarland.

10

The Truth About Friendship

I spent the next month packing. In some ways, I was sad to be leaving the city. I was used to it.

Then I thought about how great it would be to have both Mom and Dad home. And I thought about living by trees and critters. That would be pretty cool. Every day would be like our camping trip.

On my last day at school, everyone said they'd miss me. Kids always did that. It happened every time I moved.

It still surprises me, though. Especially since most of those kids wanted nothing to do with me while I was there. I guess moving away makes others feel left behind.

Finally we set off for our new home in the woods. I felt a surge of happiness. I really thought this could be a new start for me.

I looked forward to learning about things I'd never studied before—like astronomy and cougars. This time, even *I* was happy to be moving.

Soon it was my first day of school—again. Mom and I arrived at Waterton Middle School.

It was three stories tall and built out of thousands of limestone cubes. The cubes were mined right here in Waterton. The school was a mass of windows and blocks. It looked cool.

We found the office. Mom signed me up for both the regular and accelerated programs. They called the accelerated program *TAG*. That was short for "Talented and Gifted."

The Truth Test

The principal himself showed me to my science classroom. Mrs. Krupke, my science teacher, assigned me a seat. We talked a little before the bell rang. She told me I'd like it here.

The kids filed in. I looked them over, one by one. I tried hard not to be noticed. I didn't want them to know I was sizing them up.

After the bell rang, Mrs. Krupke took roll and introduced me. I was ready for her to ask me to tell about myself. But she didn't. I liked her already.

The class started reading a chapter on electricity. Then a really big kid walked through the door. He was carrying a huge box in his arms.

I stared at him. Was he a kid or an adult? I couldn't tell. He wore denim overalls, a black T-shirt that matched his hair, and tennis shoes.

"Good Morning, Cort," Mrs. Krupke said. "Why don't you put your things away. Then we'll stop for your sharing time."

Cort muttered an "okay." He balanced the large cardboard box on a desk. He unhooked his backpack and slid his books into his desk. When he finished, he began taking pieces out of the box.

What was it? I strained to see what he took out. But there were too many heads in the way.

There were some tinkering sounds of metal against metal, a little low whistle, and a gentle engine noise. Again, I swiveled on my seat to get a better look.

It was an electric train set!

I'd seen those before. I'd even seen a giant one that was used as a kiddie ride at a fair.

But I'd never known any person who had one this great. I bobbed my head up and down, left and right. I made out tiny trees, an engine house, a tunnel, and track curved into a figure eight.

Something about electrical gadgets always makes me want to try them out. I wondered how many lemons it would take to power it. And I wondered how much weight the train could pull.

It was all I could do to stay seated. I was so excited!

Cort finished setting up. He had raced the train once around the track. He announced he was ready for sharing.

Mrs. Krupke asked him to give a short presentation. Then she'd call us by rows to go back and take a better look.

"Well," he said, brushing long black bangs to one side of his forehead. "This is a model train set. I started getting pieces for my eighth birthday. Then everyone started giving me pieces for birthdays, Christmases, you name it."

He took up the control box and showed the class how it worked. "You move the lever up to make the train go forward and down to make it go backward. If you move it side to side, it releases the junctions."

The Truth Test

There were a couple of questions about how fast it could go and what else he had at home. He said he figures it tops out at about 30 miles an hour. And he said that he had an entire bedroom full of train stuff.

Mrs. Krupke began calling rows. I worked as well as I could until it was my row's turn. I followed the others, careful not to block anyone's view.

Like I said, Cort was a big kid. In fact, he was far larger than Brandon had been. I only came up to his shoulder. So I was nervous.

But he seemed calm—the quiet type. He didn't seem to be the kind of kid to be afraid of.

After everyone else asked their questions, I asked mine. I asked about the various engines for the train sets. I asked whether the train ever flew off its track and if he'd ever caused two trains to collide. Then I asked if I could take it around the track once. I had lots of questions.

Cort answered all my questions in his relaxed way. Then he offered to stay in at lunch so we could look at his train set a little longer.

I grinned. I went back to my desk and counted the minutes. I did manage to finish reading the chapter.

It was while I was reading silently that it hit me. I knew why Cort had offered to stay in!

It had to do with the book Mrs. Clevenger had read us. In one chapter, the author talked about how important it is to be interested in other people.

I found Cort's hobby truly fascinating. And it showed. So Cort was interested in me too.

I looked forward to lunch more than ever. Maybe Cort and I could be friends.

The bell rang and the kids hurried to their next class. Cort told me where my next class was and said he'd see me at lunch. The rest of my morning classes flew by.

At lunchtime, I hurried to Mrs. Krupke's room. I got there before Cort. I walked slowly over to the train set. But I didn't touch anything until Cort got there and invited me to.

We spent an enjoyable lunch making the train chug up a hill. We made it drag two plastic trees up the hill. Then we made it crush a pencil on the track by racing the train over it. It was cool.

When the bell signaled the end of lunch, Cort surprised me. "Hey," he said, "you wanna come over sometime and see my whole setup?"

My heart leaped. This was better than kicking dirt clods with Marty. "Sure," I answered.

We exchanged phone numbers later in the day. After a long bus ride home, I told my parents about Cort's train set.

They were pleased I'd made a friend so quickly. They told me I could have him over for pizza that Friday, if I'd like. I told them I would.

The Truth Test

Later that night, I phoned Cort and we made plans. On Thursday, we were going to his house to play with the train set. On Friday, we were coming to my house for pizza. We were also going to explore an old tree house in our backyard.

I lay in bed that night, thinking. Outside, the moon was shining brightly. Mars was flickering a distant red. An owl was hooting his tune. Two squirrels were chattering noisily in a tree.

They were good sounds. Despite my need for sleep, I found myself unwilling to let go of this great day. I thought about the school, the assignments, and the other kids. Everything had gone well.

Just before sleep claimed me, I remembered Mrs. Clevenger's words. Everyone contributes to a problem. And everyone contributes to the solution.

I realized I had created this good day. I had finally found the truth about making friends. It was all about being a friend first. And I didn't need a test to prove it.

About the Author

Lori Pollard-Johnson graduated from the University of Washington with a bachelor's degree in social sciences and a certificate of education. She's worked in many fields, including shoe design and importing, retail, wholesale, warehouse, and office.

Her true loves, however, are writing and teaching. In the past few years, Ms. Pollard-Johnson has concentrated all of her professional energies into these two areas. She is happiest when she finds the perfect balance between the two.

Currently, Ms. Pollard-Johnson lives outside of Wilkeson, Washington. Wilkeson is a small rural community near Seattle. Mount Rainier sits just beyond their wooded 8½ acres. A creek running on one side of their land welcomes critters of fin, hoof, and feather.

When she's not teaching or writing, Ms. Pollard-Johnson spends time with her husband Brian and two children, Kacea and Grady. She also enjoys gardening, reading, cooking, stenciling, and splashing in her creek.